NO '98

The Flat Man

Carolrhoda Books, Inc., c/o The Lerner Publishing Group
241 First Avenue North, Minneapolis, MN 55401 U.S.A.

Website address: www. lernerbooks.com

LIBRARY OF CONGRESS CATALOGING-IN-PUBLICATION DATA

Impey, Rose.
    The Flat Man / by Rose Impey ; illustrations by Moira Kemp.
      p.   cm. — (Creepies)
    Summary: At bedtime as he tries to fall asleep, a young boy has
fun scaring himself by imagining the noises he hears are coming from
the Flat Man, who is creeping up to get into bed with him.
    ISBN 1-57505-294-6 (alk. paper)
    [1. Bedtime—Fiction. 2. Monsters—Fiction. 3. Fear of the dark—
Fiction.] I. Kemp, Moira, ill. II. Title. III. Series.
PZ7.I344F1   1998
[E]—dc21 dc21
[II 1b11 12–01–97]   97–46718

Printed in Singapore
Bound in the United States of America
1 2 3 4 5 6 – O/S – 03 02 01 00 99 98

The Flat Man

by Rose Impey
illustrations by Moira Kemp

Carolrhoda Books, Inc./Minneapolis

8511446

At night when it is dark
and I am in bed
and I can't get to sleep,
I hear noises.

I hear tap, tap, tap.
I know what it is.
It's a tree blowing in the wind.
It taps on the glass.
That's all.

But I like to pretend
it's the Flat Man trying to get in.
His long, bony finger
taps on the glass.

"Let me in," he whispers.
Tap, tap, tap.

I like scaring myself.
It's only a game.

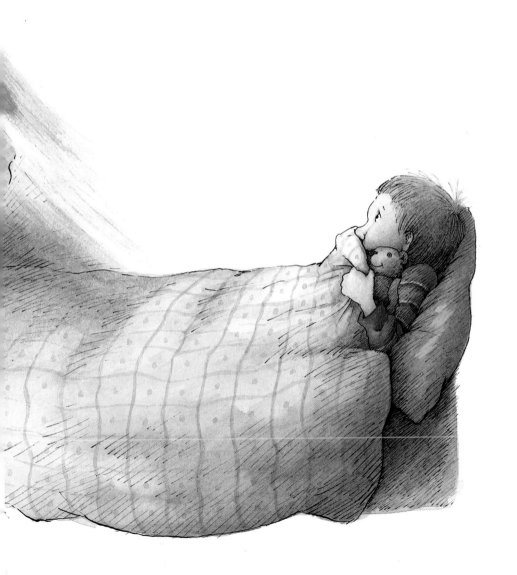

I hear rattle, rattle, rattle.
I know what it is.
A train is going by.
It makes the whole house shake
and the windows rattle,
as if its teeth are chattering.
That's what it is.

But I like to pretend
it's the Flat Man squeezing himself
as thin as he can
through the crack.

"You can't keep me out," he whispers.
Rattle, rattle, rattle.

I hear shsh, shsh, shsh.
I know what it is.
It's my baby brother
making noises in his sleep.
It sounds as if the sea's coming in.

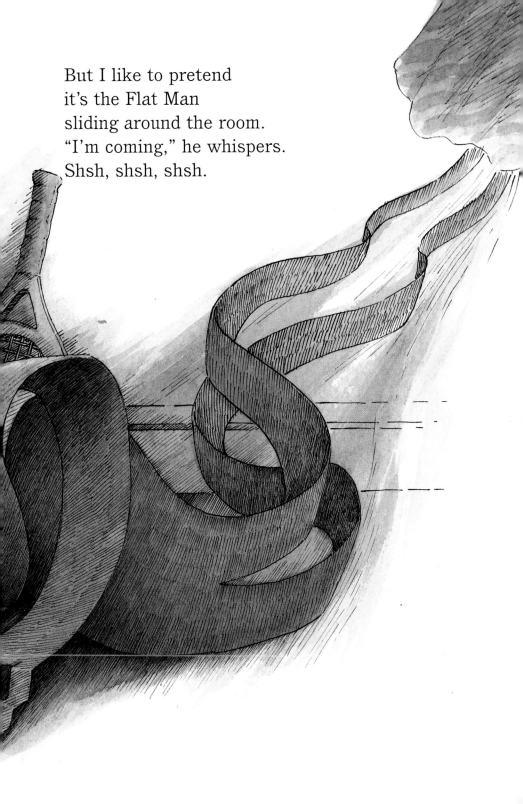

But I like to pretend
it's the Flat Man
sliding around the room.
"I'm coming," he whispers.
Shsh, shsh, shsh.

He keeps his back
close against the wall.
He clings like
a stretched-out skin.
And I know why.

I know the Flat Man's secret.
He's afraid of the light.
He hates open spaces.
That's why he creeps in corners
and drifts in the dark.

One flash of bright light
and he would shrivel up
like a crumpled piece of paper.
The slightest breeze
could blow him away.

So he slips and slides
in the shadows
until he is near my bed.
Then silently
he waits for his chance.

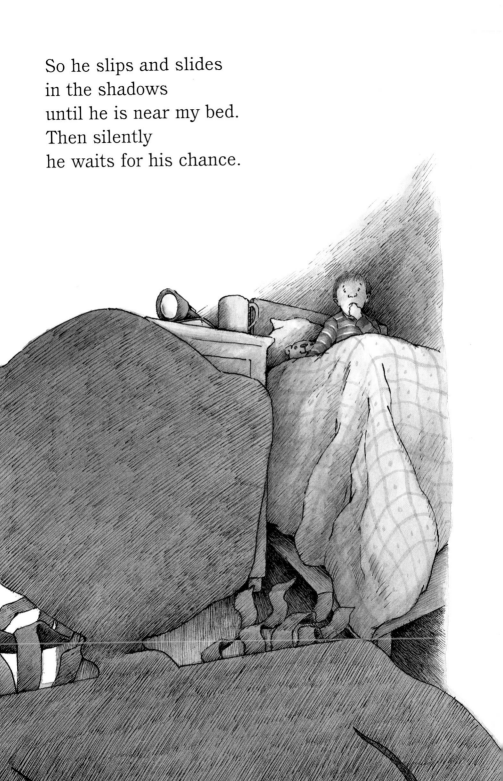

Now I can't hear a sound.
I know what that means.
There is no one there.
No one at all.

But I like to pretend
the Flat Man is holding his breath.
He is waiting
without a sound.
Listen . . .

When everything is quiet
and everything is still,
he will dart over
and slide onto my bed.

I feel a chill down my back.
I know what it is.
There is a little gap
close to the floor
where the wind blows in.
That's all.

But I pretend
it's the Flat Man
coming closer
and closer,
breathing his icy breath on me.
It makes me shiver.

I pull the covers up
and hold them tight
under my chin.
This is to stop the Flat Man
from creeping into bed with me.

But then I think to myself
he's so thin,
he could slide in the smallest crack.
He could creep in
right now . . .
without me knowing.

He could be lying there
already
by my side,
cold and flat.

I lie there afraid to move.
An icy feeling is spreading
all the way up my back.

Someone or something
seems to be wrapping itself
around my chest,

I can't breathe!
I try to think,
but my brain is racing around my head.
It won't stop.
There must be something I can do.
Suddenly I remember . . .
the Flat Man's secret!
He doesn't like to be out in the open.
He's afraid he might blow away.

I throw back the covers.
I flap them up and down
like a whirlwind.
"I'll get rid of you," I say.
Flap, flap, flap.

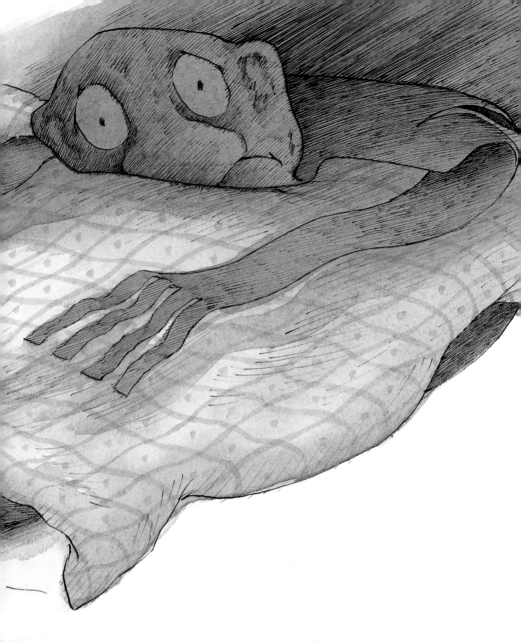

The Flat Man flies up in the air.
He is carried
struggling
across the room.

Next I jump out of bed.
I shine my flashlight at him.
"Take that . . . ," I say.

I switch on the lamp.
". . . and that . . ."
I turn on the bedroom light.
". . . and that!"
Flash, flash, flash.

I can hear the Flat Man
cry out in pain.
He starts to shrivel up.
He curls at the edges
and floats toward the window.

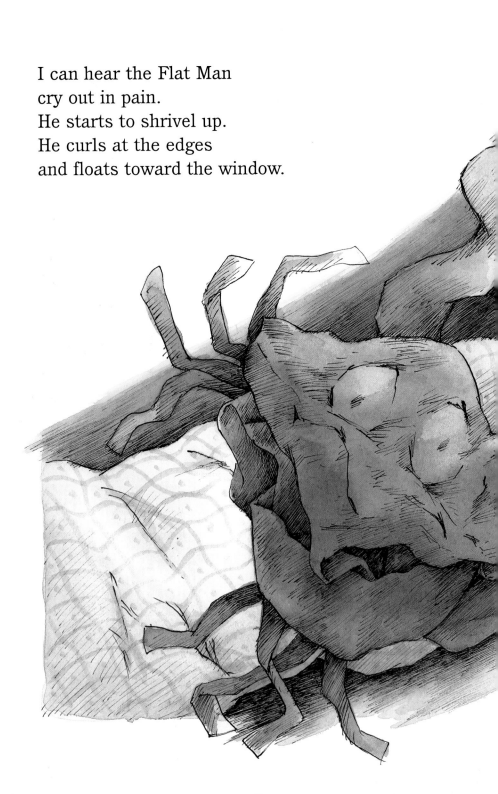

I rush to get there first.
I throw it open.
He drifts out on the wind.
He disappears into the black sky.

I close the window
so tight
not even the Flat Man can get in.
SLAM!

"Good riddance," I shout
and I make a terrible face
just in case
the Flat Man is looking back.

Suddenly my bedroom door opens.

A deep voice says,
"What on earth
do you think you're doing?"

It's my dad.
He looks at me,
making a face.
"For goodness sake,
close those curtains," he says,
"and get into bed."

I creep back.
"I was playing," I say.
"Playing?" says Dad.
"Scaring myself," I say.
"Scaring yourself?" says Dad.
"It's only a game," I say.
"Hmmm," says Dad.
"Well, I'll scare you in a minute
and that *won't* be a game."

He turns off the light.
He shuts the door
and goes downstairs.

Now it is really quiet
and dark again.
I lie in bed.
I screw up my eyes
and I can see shapes.

I can see a big black dragon on the wall.
I know what it is.
It's the kite
my grandpa brought me from China.
It hangs from the picture hook.
That's all.

But I like to pretend
it's the Flying Vampire
ready to swoop down on me . . .
Wheeeeeee!

Rose Impey worked in a bank when she first left school, but this proved to be a big mistake, so she went back to school to become a teacher instead. In addition to teaching, she reviewed, sold, and gave talks about children's books before deciding to write them herself. She has since written numerous books for children, most of which are based on her experiences either as a teacher or as a parent. Ms. Impey has two teenage daughters. When she's not reading, she enjoys swimming, reading, eating, talking, and reading her own stories aloud to children.

Moira Kemp was born in Kingston, Surrey, England. She studied history at Oxford University and art at Camberwell School of Arts and Crafts in England. She has illustrated a number of books for children, including the Helpful Betty books, published by Carolrhoda. Her children's book illustrations have been exhibited at the Barbican and the National Theatre in London.